Luna
Lovebug

Rachel Zainer

Fulton Books, Inc.
Meadville, PA

Published by Fulton Books 2021

ISBN 978-1-64952-737-0 (paperback)
ISBN 978-1-64952-738-7 (digital)

Printed in the United States of America

Luna Lovebug

Rachel D. Zaiger

There once was a girl named Luna Lovebug.
She was cuddly, and wuddly, and loved to give hugs.

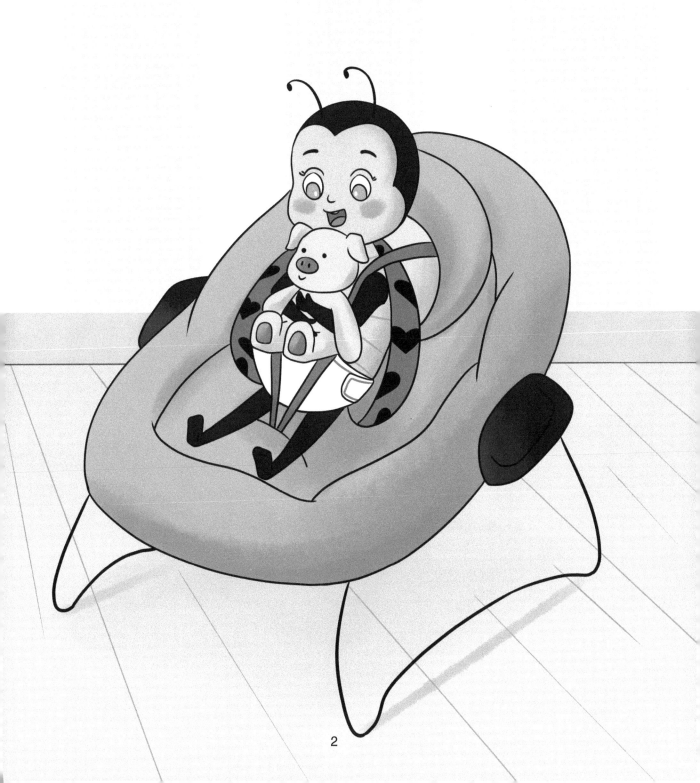

She loved her dad oh so much, she smiled at him all day.
She loved how warm he was and how they'd dance
the night away.

She loved her mom dearly, that much was quite clear.
She loved how she fed her, and held her so near.

She loved her dog Lincoln, with whom she would play.

She loved morning cuddles, she'd cuddle all day.

She loved her Grandma, who read to her lots.

Who did tummy time, and took her on long walks.

She loved her Grandpa, who held her so nice.
Who carried her around the house, and taught her
about Christ.

She loved her Nona, who gave fashion advice.

Who talked with her all day, and taught her how to play nice.

She loved her Papa, who was oh so cool.
Who had a motorcycle, and helped her dad fix stuff
with his tools.

And what she loved most of all, as you can probably
    see,
was the love and joy she had, when she spent time
    with all her family.

About the Author

Rachel Zaiger began her career as a children's author while on maternity leave. She is also a lawyer and has been published in various legal publications. She lives in Minnesota with her husband and has one child, Luna.

CPSIA information can be obtained
at www.ICGtesting.com
Printed in the USA
BVHW021924081121
621126BV00021B/512